Mystery, Inc.

BIBLIOMYSTERY SERIES

- #1 Ken Bruen, *The Book of Virtue*, $4.95
- #2 Reed Farrel Coleman, *The Book of Ghosts*, $4.95
- #3 Anne Perry, *The Scroll*, $4.95
- #4 Nelson DeMille, *The Book Case*, $6.95
- #5 C.J. Box, *Pronghorns of the Third Reich*, $4.95
- #6 William Link, *Death Leaves a Bookmark*, $4.95
- #7 Jeffery Deaver, *An Acceptable Sacrifice*, $5.95
- #8 Loren D. Estleman, *Book Club*, $4.95
- #9 Laura Lippman, *The Book Thing*, $4.95
- #10 Andrew Taylor, *The Long Sonata of the Dead*, $4.95
- #11 Peter Blauner, *The Final Testament*, $4.95
- #12 John Connolly, *The Caxton Lending Library & Book Depository*, $6.95
- #13 David Bell, *Rides a Stranger*, $4.95
- #14 Thomas H. Cook, *What's in a Name?*, $4.95
- #15 Mickey Spillane & Max Allan Collins, *It's in the Book*, $4.95
- #16 Peter Lovesey, *Remaindered*, $5.95
- #17 F. Paul Wilson *The Compendium of Srem*, $5.95
- #18 Lyndsay Faye, *The Gospel of Sheba*, $5.95
- #19 Bradford Morrow, *The Nature of My Inheritance*, $5.95
- #20 R.L. Stine, *The Sequel*, $4.95
- #21 Joyce Carol Oates, *Mystery, Inc.*, $6.95

Mystery, Inc.

By
Joyce Carol Oates

Mysterious Bookshop

New York

Mystery, Inc.
by Joyce Carol Oates

Copyright © 2014

All rights reserved. Permission to reprint,
in whole or in part,
should be addressed to:
Otto Penzler
The Mysterious Bookshop
58 Warren Street
New York, N.Y. 10007
Ottopenzler@mysteriousbookshop.com

ISBN 978-1-61316-067-1 (Limited Edition)
ISBN 978-1-61316-068-8 (Paperback)

Mystery, Inc.

I AM VERY EXCITED! For at last, after several false starts, I have chosen the perfect setting for my bibliomystery.

It is Mystery, Inc., a beautiful old bookstore in Seabrook, New Hampshire, a town of less than two thousand year-round residents overlooking the Atlantic Ocean between New Castle and Portsmouth.

For those of you who have never visited this legendary bookstore, one of the gems of New England, it is located in the historic High Street district of Seabrook, above the harbor, in a block of elegantly renovated brownstones originally built in 1888. Here are the offices of an architect, an attorney-at-law, a dental surgeon; here are shops and boutiques—leather goods, handcrafted silver jewelry, the Tartan Shop, Ralph Lauren, Esquire Bootery. At 19 High Street a weathered old sign in black and gilt creaks in the wind above the sidewalk:

> MYSTERY, INC. BOOKSELLERS
> New & Antiquarian Books,
> Maps, Globes, Art
> Since 1912

The front door, a dark-lacquered red, is not flush with the sidewalk but several steps above it; there is a broad stone stoop, and a black wrought iron railing. So that, as you stand on the sidewalk gazing at the display window, you must gaze *upward*.

Mystery, Inc. consists of four floors with bay windows on each floor that are dramatically illuminated when the store is open in the evening. On the first floor, books are displayed in the bay window with an (evident) eye for the attractiveness of their bindings: leather-bound editions of such 19th-century classics as Wilkie Collins's *The Moonstone* and *The Woman in White,* Charles Dickens's *Bleak House* and *The Mystery of Edwin Drood,* A. Conan Doyle's *The Adventures of Sherlock*

Holmes, as well as classic 20th-century mystery-crime fiction by Raymond Chandler, Dashiell Hammett, Cornell Woolrich, Ross Macdonald, and Patricia Highsmith and a scattering of popular American, British, and Scandinavian contemporaries. There is even a title of which I have never heard—*The Case of the Unknown Woman: The Story of One of the Most Intriguing Murder Mysteries of the 19th Century*, in what appears to be a decades-old binding.

As I step inside Mystery, Inc. I feel a pang of envy. But in the next instant this is supplanted by admiration—for envy is for small-minded persons.

The interior of Mystery, Inc. is even more beautiful than I had imagined. Walls are paneled in mahogany with built-in bookshelves floor to ceiling; the higher shelves are accessible by ladders on brass rollers, and the ladders are made of polished wood. The ceiling is comprised of squares of elegantly hammered tin; the floor is parquet, covered in small carpets. As I am a book collector myself—and a bookseller—I note how attractively books are displayed without seeming to overwhelm the customer; I see how cleverly books are positioned upright to intrigue the eye; the customer is made to feel welcome as in an old-fashioned library with leather chairs and sofas scattered casually about. Here and there against the walls are glass-fronted cabinets containing rare and first-edition books, no doubt under lock and key. I do feel a stab of envy, for of the mystery bookstores I own, in what I think of as my modest mystery-bookstore empire in New England, not one is of the class of Mystery, Inc., or anywhere near.

In addition, it is Mystery, Inc.'s online sales that present the gravest competition to a bookseller like myself, who so depends upon such sales . . .

Shrewdly I have timed my arrival at Mystery, Inc. for a half-hour before closing time, which is 7 P.M. on Thursdays, and hardly likely to be crowded. (I think there are only a few other customers—at least on the first floor, within my view.) In this wintry season dusk has begun as early as 5:30 PM. The air is wetly cold, so that the lenses of my glasses are covered with a fine film of steam; I am vigorously polishing them when a young woman salesclerk with tawny gold, shoulder-length hair approaches me to ask if I am looking for anything in particular, and I tell her that I am just browsing, thank you—"Though I would like to meet the proprietor of this beautiful store, if he's on the premises."

The courteous young woman tells me that her employer, Mr. Neuhaus, is in the store, but upstairs in his office; if I am interested in some of the special collections or antiquarian holdings, she can call him . . .

"Thank you! I am interested indeed but just for now, I think I will look around."

What a peculiar custom it is, the *openness of a store*. Mystery, Inc. might contain hundreds of thousands of dollars of precious merchandise; yet the door is unlocked, and anyone can step inside from the street into the virtually deserted store, carrying a leather attaché case in hand, and smiling pleasantly.

It helps of course that I am obviously a gentleman. And one might guess, a book-collector and book-lover.

As the trusting young woman returns to her computer at the check-out counter, I am free to wander about the premises. Of course, I will avoid the other customers.

I am impressed to see that the floors are connected by spiral staircases, and not ordinary utilitarian stairs; there is a small elevator at the rear which doesn't tempt me as I suffer from mild claustrophobia. (Being locked in a dusty closet as a child by a sadistic older brother surely is the root of this phobia, which I have managed to disguise from most people who know me, including my bookstore employees who revere me, I believe, for being a frank, forthright, commonsensical sort of man free of any sort of neurotic compulsion!) The first floor of Mystery, Inc. is American books; the second floor is British and foreign-language books, and Sherlock Holmesiana (an entire rear wall); the third floor is first editions, rare editions, and leatherbound sets; the fourth floor is maps, globes, and antiquarian art-works associated with mayhem, murder, and death.

It is here on the fourth floor, I'm sure, that Aaron Neuhaus has his office. I can imagine that his windows overlook a view of the Atlantic, at a short distance, and that the office is beautifully paneled and furnished.

I am feeling nostalgic for my old habit of *book theft*—when I'd been a penniless student decades ago, with a yearning for books. The thrill of thievery—and the particular reward, a *book*! In fact for years my most prized possessions were books stolen from Manhattan bookstores along Fourth Avenue that had no great monetary value—only just the satisfaction of being *stolen*. Ah, those days before security cameras!

Of course, there are security cameras on each floor of Mystery, Inc. If my plan is successfully executed, I will remove the tape and destroy it; if not, it will not matter that my likeness will be preserved on the tape for a few weeks, then destroyed. In fact I am *lightly disguised*—these whiskers are not mine, and the black-plastic-framed tinted glasses I am wearing are very different than my usual eyeglasses.

Just before closing time at Mystery, Inc. there are only a few customers, whom I intend to outstay. One or two on the first floor; a solitary individual on the second floor perusing shelves of Agatha Christie; a middle-aged couple on the third floor looking for a birthday present for a relative; an older man on the fourth floor perusing the art on the walls—reproductions of fifteenth century German woodcuts titled "Death and the Maiden," "The Dance of Death," and "The Triumph of Death"—macabre lithographs of Picasso,

Munch, Schiele, Francis Bacon—, reproductions of Goya's "Saturn Devouring His Children," "Witches' Sabbath," and "The Dog." (Too bad it would be imprudent of me to strike up a conversation with this gentleman, whose taste in macabre art-work is very similar to my own, judging by his absorption in Goya's Black Paintings!) I am indeed admiring—it is remarkable that Aaron Neuhaus can sell such expensive works of art in this out-of-the-way place in Seabrook, New Hampshire, in the off-season.

By the time I descend to the first floor, most of these customers have departed; the final customer is making a purchase at the check-out counter. To bide my time, I take a seat in one of the worn old leather chairs that seems almost to be fitted to my buttocks; so comfortable a chair, I could swear it was my own, and not the property of Aaron Neuhaus. Close by is a glass-fronted cabinet containing first editions of novels by Raymond Chandler—quite a treasure trove! There is a virtual *itch* to my fingers in proximity to such books.

I am trying not to feel embittered. I am trying simply to feel *competitive*—this is the American way!

But it's painfully true—not one of my half-dozen mystery bookstores is so well-stocked as Mystery, Inc., or so welcoming to visitors; at least two of the more recently acquired stores are outfitted with ugly utilitarian fluorescent lights which give me a headache, and fill me with despair. Virtually none of my customers are so affluent-appearing as the customers here in Mystery, Inc., and their taste in mystery fiction is limited primarily to predictable, formulaic bestsellers—you would not see shelves devoted to Ellery Queen in a store of mine, or an entire glass-fronted case of Raymond Chandler's first editions, or a wall of Holmesiana. My better stores carry only a few first editions and antiquarian books—certainly, no art-works! Nor do I seem able to hire attractive, courteous, intelligent employees like this young woman—perhaps because I can't afford to pay them much more than the minimum wage, and so they have no compunction about quitting abruptly.

In my comfortable chair it is gratifying to overhear the friendly conversation between this customer and the young woman clerk, whose name is Laura—for, if I acquire Mystery, Inc., I will certainly want to keep attractive young Laura on the staff as my employee; if necessary, I will pay her just slightly more than her current salary, to insure that she doesn't quit.

When Laura is free, I ask her if I might examine a first-edition copy of Raymond Chandler's *Farewell My Lovely*. Carefully she unlocks the cabinet, and removes the book for me—its publication date is 1940, its dust jacket in good, if not perfect, condition, and the price is $1,200. My heart gives a little leap—I already have one copy of this Chandler novel, for which, years ago, I paid much less; at the present time, in one of my better stores, or online, I could possibly resell it for $1,500 . . .

"This is very attractive! Thank you! But I have a few questions, I wonder if I might speak with . . ."

"I will get Mr. Neuhaus. He will want to meet *you*."

Invariably, at independently owned bookstores, proprietors are apt to want to meet customers like *me*.

Rapidly I am calculating—how much would Aaron Neuhaus's widow ask for this property? Indeed, how much is this property worth, in Seabrook? New Hampshire has suffered from the current, long-term recession through New England, but Seabrook is an affluent coastal community whose population more than quadruples in the summer, and so the bookstore may be worth as much as $800,000 . . . Having done some research, I happen to know that Aaron Neuhaus owns the property outright, without a mortgage. He has been married, and childless, for more than three decades; presumably, his widow will inherit his estate. As I've learned from past experiences, widows are notoriously vulnerable to quick sales of property; exhausted by the legal and financial responsibilities that follow a husband's death, they are eager to be free of encumbrances, especially if they know little about finances and business. Unless she has children and friends to advise her, a particularly distraught widow is capable of making some very unwise decisions.

Dreamily, I have been holding the Raymond Chandler first edition in my hands without quite seeing it. The thought has come to me—*I must have Mystery, Inc. It will be the jewel of my empire.*

"Hello?"—here is Aaron Neuhaus, standing before me.

Quickly I rise to my feet and thrust out my hand to be shaken—"Hello! I'm very happy to meet you. My name is—" As I proffer Neuhaus my invented name I feel a wave of heat lifting into my face. Almost, I fear that Neuhaus has been observing me at a little distance, reading my most secret thoughts while I'd been unaware of him.

He knows me. But—he cannot know me.

As Aaron Neuhaus greets me warmly it seems clear that the proprietor of Mystery, Inc. is not at all suspicious of this stranger who has introduced himself as "Charles Brockden." Why would he be? There are no recent photographs of me, and no suspicious reputation has accrued to my invented name; indeed, no suspicious reputation has accrued about my actual name as the owner of a number of small mystery bookstores in New England.

Of course, I have studied photographs of Aaron Neuhaus. I am surprised that Neuhaus is so youthful, and his face so unlined, at sixty-three.

Like any enthusiastic bookseller, Neuhaus

is happy to answer my questions about the Chandler first edition and his extensive Chandler holdings; from this, our conversation naturally spreads to other, related holdings in his bookstore—first editions of classic mystery-crime novels by Hammett, Woolrich, James M. Cain, John D. MacDonald, and Ross Macdonald, among others. Not boastfully but matter-of-factly Neuhaus tells me that he owns one of the two or three most complete collections of published work by the pseudonymous "Ellery Queen"—including novels published under other pseudonyms and magazines in which Ellery Queen stories first appeared. With a pretense of naïveté I ask how much such a collection would be worth—and Aaron Neuhaus frowns and answers evasively that the worth of a collection depends upon the market and he is hesitant to state a fixed sum.

This is a reasonable answer. The fact is, any collectors' items are worth what a collector will pay for them. The market may be inflated, or the market may be deflated. All prices of all things—at least, useless beautiful things like rare books—are inherently absurd, rooted in the human imagination and in the all-too-human predilection to desperately want what others value highly, and to scorn what others fail to value. Unlike most booksellers in our financially distressed era, Aaron Neuhaus has had so profitable a business he doesn't need to sell in a deflated market but can hold onto his valuable collections—indefinitely, it may be!

These, too, the wife will inherit. So I am thinking.

The questions I put to Aaron Neuhaus are not duplicitous but sincere—if somewhat naïve-sounding—for I am very interested in the treasures of Aaron Neuhaus's bookstore, and I am always eager to extend my bibliographical knowledge.

Soon, Neuhaus is putting into my hands such titles as *A Bibliography of Crime & Mystery Fiction 1749-1990*; *Malice Domestic: Selected Works of William Roughead, 1889-1949*; *My Life in Crime: A Memoir of a London Antiquarian Bookseller (1957)*; *The Mammoth Encyclopedia of Modern Crime Fiction*; and an anthology edited by Aaron Neuhaus, *One Hundred and One Best American Noir Stories of the 20th Century*. All of these are known to me, though I have not read one of them in its entirety; Neuhaus's *One Hundred and One Best American Noir Stories* is one of the backlist bestsellers in most of my stores. To flatter Neuhaus I tell him that I want to buy his anthology, along with the Chandler first edition—"And maybe something else, besides. For I have to confess, I seem to have fallen in love with your store."

At these words a faint flush rises into Neuhaus's face. The irony is, they are quite sincere words even as they are coolly intended to manipulate the bookseller.

Neuhaus glances at his watch—not because he's hoping that it's nearing 7 P.M., and time to close his store, but rather because he hopes he has more time to spend with this very promising customer.

Soon, as booksellers invariably do, Aaron Neuhaus will ask his highly promising customer if he can stay a while, past closing-time; we might adjourn to his office, to speak more comfortably, and possibly have a drink.

Each time, it has worked this way. Though there have been variants, and my first attempt at each store wasn't always successful, necessitating a second visit, this has been the pattern.

Bait, bait taken.

Prey taken.

Neuhaus will send his attractive sales clerk home. The last glimpse Laura will have of her (beloved?) employer will be a pleasant one, and her recollection of the last customer of the day—(the last customer of Neuhaus's life)—will be vivid perhaps, but misleading. *A man with ginger-colored whiskers, black plastic-framed glasses, maybe forty years old—or fifty... Not tall, but not short... Very friendly.*

Not that anyone will suspect *me*. Even the brass initials on my attaché case—*CB*—have been selected to mislead.

Sometime this evening Aaron Neuhaus will be found dead in his bookstore, very likely his office, of natural causes, presumably of a heart attack—if there is an autopsy. (He will be late to arrive home: his distraught wife will call. She will drive to Mystery, Inc. to see what has happened to him and/or she will call 911 to report an emergency long after the "emergency" has expired.) There could be no reason to think that an ordinary-seeming customer who'd arrived and departed hours earlier could have had anything to do with such a death.

Though I am a wholly rational person, I count myself one of those who believe that some individuals are so personally vile, so disagreeable, and make the world so much less pleasant a place, it is almost our duty to eradicate them. (However, I have not acted upon this impulse, yet—my eradications are solely in the service of business, as I am a practical-minded person.)

Unfortunately for me, however, Aaron Neuhaus is a very congenial person, exactly the sort of person I would enjoy as a friend— if I could afford the luxury of friends. He is soft-spoken yet ardent; he knows everything about mystery-detective fiction, but isn't overbearing; he listens closely, and never interrupts; he laughs often. He is of moderate height, about five feet nine or ten, just slightly taller than I am, and not quite so heavy as I am. His clothes are of excellent quality but slightly shabby, and mismatched: a dark brown Harris tweed sport coat, a red cashmere vest over a pale beige shirt, russet-brown corduroy trousers. On his feet, loafers. On his left hand, a plain gold wedding band. He has a sweetly disarming smile that offsets, to a degree, something chilly and Nordic in his gray-green gaze, which most people (I think) would not notice. His hair is a steely gray, thinning at the crown and curly at the sides, and his face is agreeably youthful. He is rather straight-backed, a little stiff, like one who has injured his back and moves cautiously to avoid pain. (Probably no one would notice this except one like myself who is by nature sharp-eyed, and has had bouts of back pain himself.)

Of course, before embarking up the coast to Seabrook, New Hampshire, in my (ordinary-seeming, unostentatious) vehicle, attaché case on the seat beside me, and plan for the elimination of a major rival memorized in every detail, I did some minimal research into my subject who has the reputation, in bookselling and antiquarian circles, of being a person who is both friendly and social and yet values his privacy highly; it is held to be somewhat perverse that many of Neuhaus's male friends have never met his wife, who has been a public school teacher in Glastonberry, N.H. for many years. (Dinner invitations to Neuhaus and his wife, from residents in Seabrook, are invariably declined "with regret.") Neuhaus's wife is said to be his high school sweetheart whom he first met in 1965 and married in 1977, in Clarksburg, N.C. So many years—faithful to one woman! It may be laudable in many men, or it may bespeak a failure of imagination and courage, but in Aaron Neuhaus it strikes me as exasperating, like Neuhaus's success with his bookstore, as if the man has set out to make the rest of us appear callow.

What I particularly resent is the fact that Aaron Neuhaus was born to a well-to-do North Carolina family, in 1951; having inherited large property holdings in Clarksburg County, N.C., as well as money held for him in trust until the age of twenty-one, he has been able to finance his bookstore(s) without the fear of bankruptcy that haunts the rest of us.

Nor was Neuhaus obliged to attend a large, sprawling, land-grant university as I did, in dreary, flat Ohio, but went instead to the prestigious, white-column'd University of Virginia, where he majored in such dilettantish subjects as classics and philosophy. After graduation Neuhaus remained at Virginia, earning a master's degree in English with a thesis titled *The Aesthetics of Deception: Ratiocination,*

Madness, and the Genius of Edgar Allan Poe, which was eventually published by the University of Virginia Press. The young Neuhaus might have gone on to become a university professor, or a writer, but chose instead to apprentice himself to an uncle who was a (renowned, much-respected) antiquarian bookseller in Washington, D.C. Eventually, in 1980, having learned a good deal from his uncle, Neuhaus purchased a bookstore on Bleecker Street, New York City, which he managed to revitalize; in 1982, with the sale of this bookstore, he purchased a shop in Seabrook, N.H., which he renovated and refashioned as a chic, upscale, yet "historic" bookstore in the affluent seaside community. All that I have learned about Neuhaus as a businessman is that he is both "pragmatic" and "visionary"— an annoying contradiction. What I resent is that Neuhaus seems to have weathered financial crises that have sent other booksellers into despair and bankruptcy, whether as a result of shrewd business dealings or—more likely— the unfair advantage an independently well-to-do bookseller has over booksellers like myself with a thin profit margin and a fear of the future. *Though I do not hate Aaron*

Neuhaus, I do not approve of such an unfair advantage—it is contrary to Nature. By now, Neuhaus might have been out of business, forced to scramble to earn a living in the aftermath of, for instance, those hurricanes of recent years that have devastated the Atlantic coastline and ruined many small businesses.

But if Mystery, Inc. suffers storm damage, or its proprietor loses money, it does not matter—there is the *unfair advantage* of the well-to-do over the rest of us.

I want to accuse Aaron Neuhaus: "How do you think you would do if our 'playing field' were level—if you couldn't bankroll your bookstore in hard times, as most of us can't? Do you think you would be selling Picasso lithographs upstairs, or first editions of Raymond Chandler; do you think you would have such beautiful floor-to-ceiling shelves, leather chairs and sofas? Do you think you would be such a naïve, gracious host, opening your store to a ginger-whiskered predator?"

It is difficult to feel indignation over Aaron Neuhaus, however, for the man is so damned *congenial*. Other rival booksellers haven't been nearly so pleasant, or, if pleasant, not nearly so well-informed and intelligent about their trade, which has made my task less of a challenge in the past.

The thought comes to me—*Maybe we could be friends? Partners? If...*

It is just 7 P.M. In the near distance a church bell tolls—unless it is the dull crashing surf of the Atlantic a quarter-mile away.

Aaron Neuhaus excuses himself, and goes to speak with his young woman clerk. Without seeming to be listening I hear him tell her that she can go home now, he will close up the store himself tonight.

Exactly as I have planned. But then, such *bait* has been dangled before.

Like any predator I am feeling excited—there is a pleasurable surge of adrenaline at the prospect of what will come next, very likely within the hour.

Timing is of the essence! All predators/hunters know this.

But I feel, too, a stab of regret. Seeing how the young blond woman smiles at Aaron Neuhaus, it is clear that she reveres her employer—perhaps loves him? Laura is in her mid-twenties, possibly a college student working part-time. Though it seems clear that there is no (sexual, romantic) intimacy between them, she might admire Neuhaus as an older man, a fatherly presence in her life; it will be terribly upsetting to her if something happens to him . . . When I acquire Mystery, Inc., I will certainly want to spend time in this store. It is not far-fetched to imagine that I might take Aaron Neuhaus's place in the young woman's life.

As the new owner of Mystery, Inc., I will not be wearing these gingery-bristling whiskers. Nor these cumbersome black plastic-framed glasses. I will look younger, and more attractive. I have been told that I resemble the great film actor James Mason . . . Perhaps I will wear Harris tweeds, and red cashmere sweater vests. Perhaps I will go on a strenuous diet, jogging along the ocean each morning, and will lose fifteen pounds. I will commiserate with Laura—*I did not know your late employer but 'Aaron Neuhaus' was the most highly regarded of booksellers—and gentlemen. I am so very sorry for your loss, Laura!*

Certainly I will want to rent living quarters in Seabrook, or even purchase property in this beautiful spot. At the present time, I move from place to place—like a hermit crab that occupies the empty shells of other sea creatures with no fixed home of its own. After acquiring an old, quasi-legendary mystery bookstore in Providence, Rhode Island, a few years ago, I lived in Providence for a while overseeing the store, until I could entrust a manager to oversee it; after acquiring a similar store in Westport, Connecticut, I lived there for a time; most recently I've been living in Boston, trying to revive a formerly prestigious mystery bookstore on Beacon Street. One would think that Beacon Street would be an excellent location for a quality mystery bookstore, and so it is—in theory; in reality, there is too much competition from other bookstores in the area. And of course there is too much competition from online sales, as from the damned, unspeakable Amazon.

I would like to ask Aaron Neuhaus how he deals with book theft, the plague of my urban-area stores, but I know the answer would be dismaying—Neuhaus's affluent customers hardly need to steal.

When Aaron Neuhaus returns, having sent the young woman home, he graciously asks if I would like to see his office upstairs. And would I like a cup of cappuccino?

"As you see, we don't have a café here. People have suggested that a café would help book sales but I've resisted—I'm afraid I am just too old-fashioned. But for special customers, we do have coffee and cappuccino—and it's very good, I can guarantee."

Of course, I am delighted. My pleasurable surprise at my host's invitation is not feigned.

In life, there are predators, and prey. A predator may require *bait*, and prey may mistake *bait* for sustenance.

In my leather attaché case is an arsenal of subtle weaponry. It is a truism that the most skillful murder is one that isn't detected as *murder* but simply *natural death*.

To this end, I have cultivated toxins as the least cumbersome and showy of murder weapons, as they are, properly used, the most reliable. I am too fastidious for bloodshed, or for any sort of violence; it has always been my feeling that violence is *vulgar*. I abhor loud noises, and witnessing the death throes of an innocent person would be traumatic for me. Ideally, I am nowhere near my prey when he (or she) is stricken by death, but miles away, and hours or even days later. There is never any apparent connection between the subject of my campaign and me—of course, I am far too shrewd to leave "clues" behind. In quasi-public places like bookstores, fingerprints are general and could never be identified or traced; but if necessary, I take time to wipe my prints with a cloth soaked in alcohol. I am certainly not obsessive or compulsive, but I am *thorough*. Since I began my (secret, surreptitious) campaign of eliminating rival booksellers in the New England area nine years ago, I have utilized poisoned hypodermic needles; poisoned candles; poisoned (Cuban) cigars; poisoned sherry, liqueur, and whiskey; poisoned macaroons; and poisoned chocolates—all with varying degrees of success.

That is, in each case my campaign was successful. But several campaigns required more than one attempt and exacted a strain on nerves already strained by economic anxieties. In one unfortunate instance, after I'd managed to dispose of the bookseller, the man's heirs refused to sell the property though I'd made them excellent offers . . . It is a sickening thing to think that one has expended so much energy in a futile project and that a wholly innocent party has died in vain; nor did I have the heart to return to that damned bookstore in Montclair, New Jersey, and take on the arrogant heirs as they deserved.

The method I have selected to dispatch the proprietor of Mystery, Inc. is one that has worked well for me in the past: chocolate truffles injected with a rare poison extracted from a Central American flowering plant bearing small red fruits like cranberries. The juice of these berries is so highly toxic, you dare not touch the outside of the berries; if the juice gets onto your skin it will burn savagely, and if it gets into your eyes—the very iris is horribly burnt away, and total blindness follows. In preparing the chocolates, which I carefully injected with a hypodermic needle, I wore not one but two pairs of surgical gloves; the operation was executed in a deep sink in a basement that could then be flooded with disinfectant and hot water. About three-quarters of the luxury chocolates have been injected with poison and the others remain untouched in their original Lindt box, in case the bearer of the luxury chocolates is obliged to sample some portion of his gift.

This particular toxin, though very potent, is said to have virtually no taste, and it has no color discernible to the naked eye. As soon as it enters the blood stream and is taken to the brain, it begins a virulent and irrevocable assault upon the central nervous system: within minutes the subject will begin to experience tremors and mild paralysis; consciousness will fade to a comatose state; by degrees, over a period of several hours, the body's organs cease to function; at first slowly, then rapidly, the lungs collapse and the heart ceases to beat; finally, the brain is struck blank and is annihilated. If there is an observer it will appear to him—or her—as though the afflicted one has had a heart attack or stroke; the skin is slightly clammy, not fevered; and there is no expression of pain or even discomfort, for the toxin is a paralytic, and thus merciful. There are no wrenching stomach pains, hideous vomiting as in the case of cyanide or poisons that affect the gastric-intestinal organs; stomach contents, if autopsied, will yield no information. The predator can observe his prey ingesting the toxin and can escape well in time to avoid witnessing even mild discomfort; it is advised that the predator take away with him his poisoned gift, so that there will be no detection. (Though this particular poison is all but undetectable by coroners and pathologists. Only a chemist who knew exactly what he was testing for could discover and identify this rare poison.) The aromatic lavender poisoned candles I'd left with my single female victim, a gratingly flirtatious bookseller in New Hope, Pennsylvania, had to work their dark magic in my absence and may have sickened, or even killed, more victims than were required... No extra poisoned cigars should be left behind, of course; and poisoned alcoholic drinks should be borne prudently away. Though it isn't likely that the poison would be discovered, there is no point in being careless.

My gracious host Aaron Neuhaus takes me to the fourth floor of Mystery, Inc. in a small elevator at the rear of the store that moves with the antique slowness of a European elevator; by breathing deeply, and trying not to think of the terrible darkness of that long-ago closet in which my cruel brother locked me, I am able to withstand a mild onslaught of claustrophobia. Only a thin film of perspiration on my forehead might betray my physical distress, if Aaron Neuhaus were to take particular notice; but, in his affably entertaining way, he is telling me about the history of Mystery, Inc.—"Quite a fascinating history, in fact.

Someday, I must write a memoir along the lines of the classic *My Life in Crime*."

On the fourth floor Aaron Neuhaus asks me if I can guess where his office door is—and I am baffled at first, staring from one wall to another, for there is no obvious sign of a door. Only by calculating where an extra room must be, in architectural terms, can I guess correctly: between reproductions of Goya's Black Paintings, unobtrusively set in the wall, is a panel that exactly mimics the room's white walls that Aaron Neuhaus pushes inward with a boyish smile.

"Welcome to my *sanctum sanctorum*! There is another, purely utilitarian office downstairs, where the staff works. Very few visitors are invited *here*."

I feel a frisson of something like dread, and the deliciousness of dread, passing so close to Goya's icons of Hell.

But Aaron Neuhaus's office is warmly lighted and beautifully furnished, like the drawing room of an English country gentleman; there is even a small fire blazing in a fireplace. Hardwood floor, partly covered in an old, well-worn yet still elegant Chinese carpet. One wall is solid books, but very special, well-preserved antiquarian books; other walls are covered in framed art-works including an oil painting by Albert Pinkham Ryder that must have been a study for the artist's famous "The Race Track" ("Death on a Pale Horse")—that dark-hued, ominous and yet beautiful oil painting by the most eccentric of nineteenth-century artists. A single high window overlooks, at a little distance, the rough waters of the Atlantic that appear in moonlight like shaken foil—the very view of the ocean I'd imagined Aaron Neuhaus might have.

Neuhaus's desk is made of dark, durable mahogany, with many drawers and pigeonholes; his chair is an old-fashioned swivel chair, with a well-worn crimson cushion. The desk top is comfortably cluttered with papers, letters, galleys, books; on it are a Tiffany lamp of exquisite colored glass and a life-sized carved ebony raven—no doubt a replica of Poe's Raven. (On the wall above the desk is a daguerreotype of Edgar Allan Poe looking pale-skinned and dissolute, with melancholy eyes and drooping mustache; the caption is *Edgar Allan Poe Creator of C. Auguste Dupin 1841*.)

Unsurprisingly, Neuhaus uses fountain

pens, not ballpoint; he has an array of colored pencils, and an old-fashioned eraser. There is even a brass letter-opener in the shape of a dagger. On such a desk, Neuhaus's state-of-the-art console computer appears out of place as a sleek, synthetic monument in an historic graveyard.

"Please sit, Charles! I will start the cappuccino machine and hope the damned thing will work. It is very Italian—*temperamental*."

I take a seat in a comfortable, well-worn leather chair facing Neuhaus's desk and with a view of the fireplace. I have brought my attaché case with the brass initials *CB*, to rest on my knees. Neuhaus fusses with his cappuccino machine, which is on a table behind his desk; he prefers cappuccino made with Bolivian coffee and skim milk, he says. "I have to confess to a mild addiction. There's a Starbucks in town but their cappuccino is nothing like mine."

Am I nervous? Pleasurably nervous? At the moment, I would prefer a glass of sherry to cappuccino!

My smile feels strained, though I am sure Aaron Neuhaus finds it affable, innocent. It is one of my stratagems to ply a subject with questions, to deflect any possible suspicion away from me, and Neuhaus enjoys answering my questions which are intelligent and well-informed, yet not overly intelligent and well-informed. The bookseller has not the slightest suspicion that he is dealing with an ambitious rival.

He is ruefully telling me that everyone who knew him, including an antiquarian bookseller uncle in Washington, D.C., thought it was a very naïve notion to try to sell works of art in a bookstore in New Hampshire—"But I thought I would give myself three or four years, as an experiment. And it has turned out surprisingly well, especially my online sales."

Online sales. These are the sales that particularly cut into my own. Politely, I ask Neuhaus how much of his business is now online?

Neuhaus seems surprised by my question. Is it too personal? Too—*professional?* I am hoping he will attribute such a question to the naïveté of Charles Brockden.

His reply is curious—"In useless, beautiful

art-works, as in books, values wax and wane according to some unknown and unpredictable algorithm."

This is a striking if evasive remark. It is somehow familiar to me, and yet—I can't recall why. I must be smiling inanely at Aaron Neuhaus, not knowing how to reply. *Useless, beautiful... Algorithm...*

Waiting for the cappuccino to brew, Neuhaus adds another log to the fire and prods it with a poker. What a bizarre gargoyle, the handle of the poker! In tarnished brass, a peevish grinning imp. Neuhaus shows it to me with a smile—"I picked this up at an estate sale in Blue Hill, Maine, a few summers ago. Curious, isn't it?"

"Indeed, yes."

I am wondering why Aaron Neuhaus has shown this demonic little face to *me*.

Such envy I've been feeling in this cozy yet so beautifully furnished *sanctum santorum*! It is painful to recall my own business offices, such as they are, utilitarian and drab, with nothing sacred about them. Outdated computers, ubiquitous fluorescent lights, charmless furniture inherited from bygone tenants. Often in a bookstore of mine the business office is also a storage room crammed with filing cabinets, packing crates, even brooms and mops, plastic buckets and step-ladders, and a lavatory in a corner. Everywhere, stacks of books rising from the floor like stalagmites. How ashamed I would be if Aaron Neuhaus were to see one of those!

I am thinking—*I will change nothing in this beautiful place. The very fountain pens on his desk will be mine. I will simply move in.*

Seeing that he has a very admiring and very curious visitor, Aaron Neuhaus is happy to chat about his possessions. The bookseller's pride in the privileged circumstances of his life is almost without ego—as one might take pleasure in any natural setting, like the ocean outside his window. Beside the large, stark daguerreotype of Poe are smaller photographs by the surrealist photographer Man Ray, of nude female figures in odd, awkward poses. Some of them are nude torsos lacking heads—very pale, marmoreal as sculpted forms. The viewer wonders uneasily: are these human beings, or mannequins? Are they human female *corpses?* Neuhaus tells me that the Man Ray photographs are taken from the photographer's *Tresor interdite* series of the

1930s—"Most of the work is inaccessible, in private collections, and never lent to museums." Beside the elegantly sinister Man Ray photographs, and very different from them, are crudely sensational crime photographs by the American photographer Weegee, taken in the 1930s and 1940s: stark portraits of men and women in the crises of their lives, beaten, bleeding, arrested and handcuffed, shot down in the street to lie sprawled, like one well-dressed mobster, face down in their own blood.

"Weegee is the crudest of artists, but he is an artist. What is notable in such 'journalistic' art is the absence of the photographer from his work. You can't comprehend what, if anything, the photographer is thinking about these doomed people . . ."

Man Ray, yes. Weegee, no. I detest crudeness, in art as in life; but of course I don't indicate this to Aaron Neuhaus, whom I don't want to offend. The man is so boyishly enthusiastic, showing off his treasures to a potential customer.

Prominent in one of Neuhaus's glass-fronted cabinets is a complete set of the many volumes of the famous British criminologist

William Roughead—"Each volume signed by Roughead"; also bound copies of the American detective pulps *Dime Detective, Black Mask,* and a copy of *The Black Lizard Big Book of Pulps.* These were magazines in which such greats as Dashiell Hammett and Raymond Chandler published stories, Neuhaus tells me, as if I didn't know.

In fact, I am more interested in Neuhaus's collection of great works of the "Golden Era of Mystery"—signed first editions by John Dickson Carr, Agatha Christie, and S.S. Van Dine, among others. (Some of these must be worth more than five thousand dollars apiece, I would think.) Neuhaus confesses that he would be very reluctant to sell his 1888 first edition of *A Study in Scarlet* in its original paper covers (priced at $100,000), or a signed first edition of *The Return of Sherlock Holmes* (priced at $35,000); more reluctantly, his first edition of *The Hound of the Baskervilles,* inscribed and signed, with handsome illustrations of Holmes and Watson (priced at $65,000). He shows me one of his "priceless" possessions—a bound copy of the February 1827 issue of *Blackwood's Magazine* containing Thomas de Quincy's infamous essay, "On

Murder Considered as One of the Fine Arts." Yet more impressively, he has the complete four volumes of the first edition (1794) of *Mysteries of Udolpho* (priced at $10,000). But the jewel of his collection, which he will never sell, he says, unless he is absolutely desperate for money, is the 1853 first edition, in original cloth with "sepia cabinet photograph of author" of Charles Dickens's *Bleak House* (priced at $75,000), signed by Dickens in his strong, assured hand, in ink that has scarcely faded!

"But this is something that would particularly interest you, 'Charles Brockden'"— Neuhaus chuckles, carefully taking from a shelf a very old book, encased in plastic, with a loose, faded binding and badly yellowed pages—Charles Brockden Brown's *Wieland; or The Transformation: An American Tale*, 1798.

This is extraordinary! One would expect to see such a rare book under lock and key in the special collections of a great university library, like Harvard.

For a moment I can't think how to reply. Neuhaus seems almost to be teasing me. It was a careless choice of a name, I suppose— "Charles Brockden." If I'd thought about it, of course I would have realized that a bookseller would be reminded of Charles Brockden Brown.

To disguise my confusion, I ask Aaron Neuhaus how much he is asking for this rare book, and Neuhaus says, "'Asking'—? I am not 'asking' any sum at all. It is not for sale."

Again, I'm not sure how to reply. Is Neuhaus laughing at me? Has he seen through my fictitious name, as through my disguise? I don't think that this is so, for his demeanor is good-natured; but the way in which he smiles at me, as if we are sharing a joke, makes me uneasy.

It's a relief when Neuhaus returns the book to its shelf, and locks up the glass-fronted cabinets. At last, the cappuccino is ready!

All this while, the fire has been making me warm—over-warm.

The ginger-colored whiskers that cover my jaws have begun to itch.

The heavy black plastic glasses, so much more cumbersome than my preferred wire-rim glasses, are leaving red marks on the bridge of my nose. Ah, I am looking forward to tearing both whiskers and glasses from my face with a cry of relief and victory in an hour—or ninety minutes—when I am departing Seabrook in my vehicle, south along the ocean road . . .

"Charles! Take care, it's very hot."

Not in a small cappuccino cup but in a hearty coffee mug, Aaron Neuhaus serves me the pungent brewed coffee, with its delightful frothed milk. The liquid is rich, very dark, scalding-hot as he has warned. I am wondering if I should take out of my attaché case the box of Lindt chocolates to share with my host, or whether it is just slightly too soon—I don't want to arouse his suspicion. If—when—Aaron Neuhaus eats one of these potent chocolates I will want to depart soon after, and our ebullient hour together will come to an abrupt conclusion. It is foolish of me perhaps, but I am almost thinking—well, it is not very realistic, but indeed, I am thinking—*Why could we not be partners? If I introduce myself as a serious book collector, one with unerring taste (if not unlimited resources, as he seems to have)—would not Aaron Neuhaus be impressed with me? Does he not, already, like me—and trust me?*

At the same time, my brain is pragmatically pursuing the more probable course of events: if I wait until Aaron Neuhaus lapses into a coma, I could take away with me a select few of his treasures, instead of having to wait until I can purchase Mystery, Inc. Though I am not a *common thief*, it has been exciting to see such rare items on display; almost, in a sense, dangled before me, by my clueless prey. Several of the less-rare items would be all that I could dare, for it would be a needless risk to take away, for instance, the Dickens first edition valued at $79,000—just the sort of greedy error that could entrap me.

"Are you often in these parts, Charles? I don't think that I have seen you in my store before."

"No, not often. In the summer, sometimes..." My voice trails off uncertainly. Is it likely that a bookstore proprietor would see, and take note, of every customer who comes into his store? Or am I interpreting Aaron Neuhaus too literally?

"My former wife and I sometimes drove to Boothbay, Maine. I believe we passed through this beautiful town, but did not stop." My voice is somewhat halting, but certainly sincere. Blindly I continue, "I am not married now—unfortunately. My wife had been my high school sweetheart but she did not share my predilection for precious old books, I'm afraid."

Is any of this true? I am hoping only that such words have the ring of plausibility.

"I've long been a lover of mysteries—in books and in life. It's wonderful to discover a fellow enthusiast, and in such a beautiful store..."

"It is! Always a wonderful discovery. I, too, am a lover of mysteries, of course—in life as in books."

Aaron Neuhaus laughs expansively. He has been blowing on his mug of cappuccino, for it is still steaming. I am intrigued by the subtle distinction of his remark, but would require some time to ponder it—if indeed it is a significant remark, and not just casual banter.

Thoughtfully, Neuhaus continues: "It is out of the profound mystery of life that 'mystery books' arise. And, in turn, 'mystery books' allow us to see the mystery of life more clearly, from perspectives not our own."

On a shelf behind the affable bookseller's desk are photographs that I have been trying to see more clearly. One, in an antique oval frame, is of an extraordinarily beautiful, young, black-haired woman—could this be Mrs. Neuhaus? I think it must be, for in another photograph she and a youthful Aaron Neuhaus are together, in wedding finery—a most attractive couple.

There is something profoundly demoralizing about this sight—such a beautiful woman, married to this man not so very different from myself! Of course—(I am rapidly calculating, cantilevering to a new, objective perspective)—the young bride is no longer young, and would be, like her husband, in her early sixties. No doubt Mrs. Neuhaus is still quite beautiful. It is not impossible to think that, in the devastated aftermath of losing her husband, the widow might not be adverse, in time, to remarriage with an individual who shares so much of her late husband's interests, and has taken over Mystery, Inc . . . . Other photographs, surely family photos, are less interesting, though suggesting that Neuhaus is a "family man" to some degree. (If we had more time, I would ask about these personal photos; but I suppose I will find out eventually who Neuhaus's relatives are.)

Also on the shelf behind Neuhaus's desk is

what appears to be a homemade art-work—a bonsai-sized tree (fashioned from a coat hanger?)—upon which small items have been hung: a man's signet ring, a man's wristwatch, a brass belt buckle, a pocket watch with a gold chain. If I didn't know that Neuhaus had no children, I would presume that this amateurish "art" has found a place amid the man's treasures which its artistry doesn't seem to merit.

At last, the cappuccino is not so scalding. It is still hot, but very delicious. Now I am wishing badly that I'd prepared a box of macaroons, more appropriate here than chocolate truffles.

As if I have only just now recalled it, I remove the Lindt box from my attaché case. An unopened box, I suggest to Aaron Neuhaus—freshly purchased and not a chocolate missing.

(It is true, I am reluctant to hurry our fascinating conversation, but—there is a duty here that must be done.)

In a display of playful horror Neuhaus half-hides his eyes—"Chocolate truffles—my favorite chocolates—and my favorite truffles!

Thank you, Charles, but—I should not. My dear wife will expect me to be reasonably hungry for dinner." The bookseller's voice wavers, as if he is hoping to be encouraged.

"Just one chocolate won't make any difference, Aaron. And your dear wife will never know, if you don't tell her."

Neuhaus is very amusing as he takes one of the chocolate truffles—(from the first, poisoned row)—with an expression both boyishly greedy and guilty. He sniffs it with delight and seems about to bite into it—then lays it on his desk top as if temporarily, in a show of virtue. He winks at me as at a fellow conspirator—"You are quite right, my dear wife needn't know. There is much in marriage that might be kept from a spouse, for her own good. Though possibly, I should bring my wife one of these also—if you could spare another, Charles?"

"Why of course—but—take more than one . . . Please help yourself—of course."

This is disconcerting. But there is no way for me to avoid offering Neuhaus the box again, this time somewhat awkwardly, turning it so that he is led to choose a chocolate truffle out of a row of non-poisoned truffles. And I will eat one with much appetite, so that Neuhaus is tempted to eat his.

How warm I am! And these damned whiskers itching!

As if he has only just thought of it, Aaron Neuhaus excuses himself to call his wife—on an old-fashioned black dial phone, talisman of another era. He lowers his voice out of courtesy, not because he doesn't want his visitor to overhear. "Darling? Just to alert you, I will be a little late tonight. A most fascinating customer has dropped by—whom I don't want to short-change." *Most fascinating.* I am flattered by this, though saddened.

So tenderly does Neuhaus speak to his wife, I feel an almost overwhelming wave of pity for him, and for her; yet, more powerfully, a wave of envy, and anger. *Why does this man deserve that beautiful woman and her love, while I have no one—no love—at all?*

It is unjust, and it is unfair. It is intolerable.

Neuhaus tells his wife he will be home, he believes, by at least 8:30 PM. Again it is flattering to me, that Neuhaus thinks so well of me; he doesn't plan to send me away for another hour. Another wife might be annoyed by such a call, but the beautiful (and mysterious) Mrs. Neuhaus does not object. "Yes! Soon. I love you too, darling." Neuhaus unabashedly murmurs these intimate words, like one who isn't afraid to acknowledge emotion.

The chocolate truffle, like the cappuccino, is indeed delicious. My mouth waters even as I eat it. I am hoping that Neuhaus will devour his, as he clearly wants to; but he has left both truffles untouched for the moment, while he sips the cappuccino. There is something touchingly childlike in this procrastination—putting off a treat, if but for a moment. I will not allow myself to think of the awful possibility that Neuhaus will eat the unpoisoned truffle and bring the poisoned truffle home to his wife.

To avoid this, I may offer Neuhaus the entire box to take home to his wife. In that way, both the owner of Mystery, Inc. and the individual who would inherit it upon his death will depart this earth. Purchasing the store from another, less personally involved heir might be, in fact, an easier stratagem.

I have asked Aaron Neuhaus who his customers are in this out-of-the-way place, and he tells me that he has a number of "surprisingly faithful, stubbornly loyal" customers who come to his store from as far away as Boston, even New York City, in good weather at least. There are local regulars, and there are the summertime customers—"Mystery, Inc. is one of the most popular shops in town, second only to Starbucks." Still, most of his sales in the past twenty-five years have been mail-order and online; the online orders are more or less continuous, emails that come in through the night from his "considerable overseas clientele."

This is a cruel blow! I'm sure that I have *no overseas clientele* at all.

Yet it isn't possible to take offense, for Aaron Neuhaus is not boasting so much as speaking matter-of-factly. Ruefully I am thinking—*The man can't help being superior. It is ironic, he must be punished for something that is not his fault.*

Like my brother, I suppose. Who had to be punished for something that wasn't his fault: a mean-spirited soul, envious and malicious regarding *me*. Though I will regret Aaron Neuhaus's fate, I will never regret my brother's fate.

Still, Aaron Neuhaus has put off eating his chocolate truffle with admirable restraint! By this time I have had a second, and Neuhaus is preparing two more cups of cappuccino. The caffeine is having a bracing effect upon my blood. Like an admiring interviewer I am asking my host where his interest in mystery derives, and Neuhaus replies that he fell under the spell of mystery as a young child, if not an infant—"I think it had to do with my astonishment at peering out of my crib and seeing faces peering at me. Who were they? My mother whom I did not yet know was my mother—my father whom I did not yet know was my father? These individuals must have seemed like giants to me—mythic figures—as in the *Odyssey*." He pauses, with a look of nostalgia. "Our lives are odysseys, obviously—continuous, ever-unexpected adventures. Except we are not journeying home, like Odysseus, but journeying away from home inexorably, like the Hubble universe."

What is this?—"Hubble universe"? I'm not sure that I fully understand what Aaron Neuhaus is saying, but there is no doubt that my companion is speaking from the heart.

As a boy he fell under the spell of mystery

fiction—boys' adventure, Sherlock Holmes, Ellery Queen, Mark Twain's *Pudd'head Wilson*—and by the age of thirteen he'd begun reading true crime writers (like the esteemed Roughead) of the kind most readers don't discover until adulthood. Though he has a deep and enduring love for American hard-boiled fiction, his long-abiding love is for Wilkie Collins and Charles Dickens—"Writers not afraid of the role coincidence plays in our lives, and not afraid of over-the-top melodrama."

This is true. Coincidence plays far more of a role in our lives than we (who believe in free will) wish to concede. And lurid, over-the-top melodrama, perhaps a rarity in most lives, but inescapable at one time or another.

Next, I ask Aaron Neuhaus how he came to purchase his bookstore, and he tells me with a nostalgic smile that indeed it was an accident—a "marvelous coincidence"—that one day when he was driving along the coast to visit relatives in Maine, he happened to stop in Seabrook—"And there was this gem of a bookstore, right on High Street, in a row of beautiful old brownstones. The store wasn't quite as it is now, slightly rundown, and neglected, yet with an intriguing sign out front—*Mystery, Inc.: M. Rackham Books.* Within minutes I saw the potential of the store and the location, and I fell in love with something indefinable in the very air of Seabrook, New Hampshire."

At this time, in 1982, Aaron Neuhaus owned a small bookstore that specialized in mystery, detective, and crime fiction in the West Village, on Bleecker Street; though he worked in the store as many as one hundred hours a week, with two assistants, he was chafing under the burden of circumscribed space, high rent and high taxes, relentless book-theft, and a clientele that included homeless derelicts and junkies who wandered into the store looking for public lavatories or for a place to sleep. His wife yearned to move out of New York City and into the country—she had an education degree and was qualified to teach school, but did not want to teach in the New York City public school system, nor did Neuhaus want her to. And so Neuhaus made a decision almost immediately to acquire the Seabrook bookstore—"If it were humanly possible."

It was an utterly impulsive decision,

Neuhaus said. He had not even consulted with his dear wife. Yet, it was unmistakable—"Like falling in love at first sight."

The row of brownstones on High Street was impressive, but *Mystery, Inc: M. Rackham Books* was not so impressive. In the first-floor bay window were displayed the predictable bestsellers one would see in any bookstore window of the time, but here amid a scattering of dead flies; inside, most of the books were trade paperbacks with lurid covers and little literary distinction. The beautiful floor-to-ceiling mahogany bookshelves—carpentry which would cost a fortune in 1982—were in place, the hammered-tin ceiling, hardwood floors. But so far as the young bookseller could see the store offered no first editions, rare or unusual books, or art-works; the second floor was used for storage, and the upper two floors were rented out. Still, the store was ideally situated on Seabrook's main street overlooking the harbor, and it seemed likely that the residents of Seabrook were generally affluent, well-educated, and discerning.

Not so exciting, perhaps, as a store on Bleecker Street in the West Village—yet, it may be that excitement is an overrated experience if you are a serious bookseller.

"After I'd been in the store for a few minutes, however, I could feel—something . . . An atmosphere of tension like the air preceding a storm. The place was virtually deserted on a balmy spring day. There were loud voices at the rear. There came then—in a hurry—the proprietor to speak eagerly with me, like a man who is dying of loneliness. When I introduced myself as a fellow bookseller, from New York City, Milton Rackham all but seized my hand. He was a large, soft-bodied, melancholic older gentleman whose adult son worked with him, or for him. At first Rackham talked enthusiastically of books—his favorites, which included, not surprisingly, the great works of Wilkie Collins, Dickens, and Conan Doyle. Then he began to speak with more emotion of how he'd been a young professor of classics at Harvard who, with his young wife who'd shared his love for books and bookstores, decided to quit the 'sterile, self-absorbed' academic world to fulfill a life's dream of buying a bookstore in a small town and making it into a 'very special place.' Unfortunately his beloved wife had died after only a few years, and his unmarried son worked with him now in the store; in recent years, the son had become "inward, troubled, unpredictable, strange—a *brooding personality.*"

It was surprising to Neuhaus, and somewhat embarrassing, that the older bookseller should speak so openly to a stranger of these personal and painful matters. And the poor man spoke disjointedly, unhappily, lowering his voice so that his heavyset, pony-tailed son (whom Neuhaus glimpsed shelving books at the rear of the store with a particular sort of vehemence, as if he were throwing livestock into vats of steaming scalding water) might not hear. In a hoarse whisper Rackham indicated to Neuhaus that the store would soon be for sale—"To the proper buyer."

"Now, I was truly shocked. But also...excited. For I'd already fallen in love with the beautiful old brownstone, and here was its proprietor, declaring that it was for sale."

Neuhaus smiles with a look of bittersweet nostalgia. It is enviable that a man can glance back over his life, and present the crucial episodes in his life, not with pain or regret but with—nostalgia!

Next, the young visitor invited Milton Rackham to speak in private with him, in his office—"Not here: Rackham's office was on the first floor, a cubbyhole of a room containing one large, solid piece of furniture, this very mahogany desk, amid a chaos of books, galleys, boxes, unpaid bills and invoices, dust balls, and desperation"—, about the bookstore, what it might cost with or without a mortgage; when it would be placed on the market, and how soon the new owner could take possession. Rackham brandished a bottle of whiskey, and poured drinks for them in "clouded" glasses; he searched for, and eventually found, a cellophane package of stale sourballs, which he offered to his guest. It was painful to see how Rackham's hands shook. And alarming to see how the older man's mood swerved from embittered to elated, from anxious to exhilarated, as he spoke excitedly to his young visitor, often interrupting himself with laughter, like one who has not spoken with anyone in a long time. He confided in Neuhaus that he didn't trust his son—"'Not with our finances, not with book orders, not with maintaining the store, and not with my life.' He'd once been very close to the boy, as he called him, but their relationship had altered significantly since his son's fortieth birthday, for no clear reason. Unfortunately, he had no other recourse than to keep his son on at the store as he couldn't afford to pay an employee a competitive wage, and the boy, who'd dropped out of Williams College midway through his freshman year, for 'mental' reasons, would have no other employment—'It is a tragic trap, fatherhood! And my wife and I had been so happy in our innocence, long ago.'" Neuhaus shudders, recalling.

"As Rackham spoke in his lowered voice I had a sudden fantasy of the son rushing into the office swinging a hand ax at us . . . I felt absolutely chilled—terrified . . . I swear, I could see that ax . . . It was as if the bookstore were haunted by something that had not yet happened."

Haunted by something that had not yet happened. Despite the heat from the fireplace, I am feeling chilled too. I glance over my shoulder to see that the door, or rather the moving panel, is shut. No one will rush in upon us here in Aaron Neuhaus's *santum sanctorum*, wielding an ax . . .

Nervously, I have been sipping my cappuccino, which has cooled somewhat. I am finding it just slightly hard to swallow—my mouth is oddly dry, perhaps because of nerves. The taste of the cappuccino is extraordinary: rich, dark, delicious. It is the frothy milk that makes the coffee so special, Neuhaus remarks that it isn't ordinary milk but goat's milk, for a sharper flavor.

Neuhaus continues—"It was from Milton Rackham that I acquired the complete set of William Roughead which, for some eccentric reason, he'd been keeping in a cabinet at the back of the store under lock and key. I asked him why this wonderful set of books was hidden away, why it wasn't prominently displayed and for sale, and Rackham said coldly, with an air of reproach, 'Not all things in a bookseller's life are for sale, sir.' Suddenly, with no warning, the old gentleman seemed to be hostile to me. I was shocked by his tone."

Neuhaus pauses, as if he is still shocked, to a degree.

"Eventually, Rackham would reveal to me

that he was hoarding other valuable first editions—some of these I have shown you, the 'Golden Age' items, which I acquired as part of the store's stock. And the first-edition *Mysteries of Udolpho*—which in his desperation to sell he practically gave away to me. And a collection of antique maps and globes, in an uncatalogued jumble on the second floor—a collection he'd inherited, he said, from the previous bookseller. Why on earth would anyone hoard these valuable items—I couldn't resist asking—and Rackham told me, again in a hostile voice, 'We gentlemen don't wear our hearts on our sleeves, do we? Do *you*?'"

It is uncanny, when Neuhaus mimics his predecessor's voice, I seem—almost—to be hearing the voice of another.

"Such a strange man! And yet, in a way—a way I have never quite articulated to anyone, before now—Milton Rackham has come to seem to me a kind of *paternal figure* in my life. He'd looked upon me as a kind of son, or rescuer—seeing that his own son had turned against him."

Neuhaus is looking pensive, as if remembering something unpleasant. And I am feeling anxious, wishing that my companion would devour the damned chocolate truffle as he clearly wishes to do.

"Charles, it's a poor storyteller who leaps ahead of his story—but—I have to tell you, before going on, that my vision of Rackham's 'brooding' son murdering him with an ax turned out to be prophetic—that is, true. It would happen exactly three weeks to the day after I'd first stepped into the bookstore—at a time when Rackham and I were negotiating the sale of the property, mostly by phone. I was nowhere near Seabrook, and received an astounding call . . ." Neuhaus passes his hand over his eyes, shaking his head.

This is a surprising revelation! For some reason, I am quite taken aback. That a bookseller was murdered in this building, even if not in this very room, and by his own son—this is a bit of a shock.

"And so—in some way—Mystery, Inc. is haunted?"—my question is uncertain.

Neuhaus laughs, somewhat scornfully—"Haunted—now? Of course not. Mystery, Inc. is a very successful, even legendary bookstore of its kind in New England. *You* would not know that, Charles, since you are not in the trade."

These words aren't so harsh as they might seem, for Neuhaus is smiling at me as one might smile at a foolish or uninformed individual for whom one feels some affection, and is quick to forgive. And I am eager to agree—I am not in *the trade.*

"The story is even more awful, for the murderer—the deranged 'boy'—managed to kill himself also, in the cellar of the store—a very dark, dank, dungeon-like space even today, which I try to avoid as much as possible. (Talk of 'haunted'! That is the likely place, not the bookstore itself.) The hand ax was too dull for the task, it seems, so the 'boy' cut his throat with a box cutter—one of those razor-sharp objects no bookstore is without." Casually Neuhaus reaches out to pick up a box cutter, that has been hidden from my view by a stack of bound galleys on his desk; as if, for one not in the "trade," a box cutter would need to be identified. (Though I am quite familiar with box cutters it is somewhat disconcerting to see one in this elegantly furnished office—lying on Aaron Neuhaus's desk!) "Following this double tragedy, the property fell into the possession of a mortgage company, for it had been heavily mortgaged. I was able to complete the sale within a few weeks, for a quite reasonable price since no one else seemed to want it." Neuhaus chuckles grimly.

"As I'd said, I have leapt ahead of my story, a bit. There is more to tell about poor Milton Rackham that is of interest. I asked him how he'd happened to learn of the bookstore here in Seabrook and he told me of how 'purely by chance' he'd discovered the store in the fall of 1957—he'd been driving along the coast on his way to Maine and stopped in Seabrook, on High Street, and happened to see the bookstore—Slater's Mystery Books & Stationers it was called—'It was such a vision!—the bay windows gleaming in the sun, and the entire block of brownstones so attractive.' A good part of Slater's merchandise was stationery, quite high-quality stationery, and other supplies of that sort, but there was an excellent collection of books as well, hardcover and paperback; not just the usual popular books but somewhat esoteric titles as well, by Robert W. Chambers, Bram Stoker, M.R. James, Edgar Wallace, Oscar Wilde (*Salome*), H P. Lovecraft. Slater seemed to have been a particular admirer of Erle Stanley Gardner, Rex Stout, Josephine Tey, and Dorothy L. Sayers, writers whom Milton Rackham admired also. The floor-to-ceiling mahogany bookshelves were in place—cabinetry that would cost a fortune at the time, as Rackham remarked again. And there were odd, interesting things stocked in the store like antique maps, globes—'A kind of treasure trove, as in an older relative's attic in which you might spend long rainy afternoons under a spell.' Rackham told me that he wandered through the store with 'mounting excitement'—feeling that it was already known to him, in a way; through a window, he looked out toward the Atlantic Ocean, and felt the 'thrill of its great beauty.' Indeed, Milton Rackham would tell me that it had been 'love at first sight'—as soon as he'd glimpsed the bookstore.

"As it turned out, Amos Slater had been contemplating selling the store, which had been a family inheritance; though, as he said, he continued to 'love books and bookselling,' it was no longer with the passion of youth, and so he hoped to soon retire. Young Milton Rackham was stunned by this good fortune. Three weeks later, with his wife's enthusiastic support, he made an offer to Amos Slater for the property, and the offer was accepted almost immediately."

Neuhaus speaks wonderingly, like a man who is recounting a somewhat fantastical tale he hopes his listeners will believe, for it is important for them to believe it.

"'My wife had a faint premonition'—this is Milton Rackham speaking—'that something might be wrong, but I paid no attention. I was heedless then, in love with my sweet young wife, and excited by the prospect of walking away from pious Harvard—(where it didn't look promising that I would get tenure)—and taking up a purer life, as I thought it, in the booksellers' trade. And so, Mildred and I arranged for a thirty-year mortgage, and made our initial payment through the Realtor, and on our first visit to the store as the new owners—when Amos Slater presented us with the keys to the building—it happened that my wife innocently asked Amos Slater how he'd come to own the store, and Amos told her a most disturbing tale, like one eager to get something off his chest . . .

"'Slater's Books'—this is Amos Slater

speaking, as reported by Milton Rackham to me—'had been established by his grandfather Barnabas in 1912. Slater's grandfather was a 'lover of books, rather than humankind'—though one of his literary friends was Ambrose Bierce who'd allegedly encouraged Barnabas's writing of fiction. Slater told Rackham a bizarre tale that at the age of eleven he'd had a 'powerful vision'—dropping by his grandfather's bookstore one day after school, he'd found the store empty—'No customers, no sales clerks, and no Grandfather, or so I thought. But then, looking for Grandfather, I went into the cellar—I turned on a light and—there was Grandfather hanging from a beam, his body strangely straight, and very still; and his face turned mercifully from me, though there was no doubt who it was. For a long moment I stood paralyzed—I could not believe what I was seeing. I could not even scream, I was so frightened . . . My grandfather Barnabas and I had not been close. Grandfather had hardly seemed to take notice of me except sneeringly—'Is it a little boy, or a little girl? *What is it?*' Grandfather Slater was a strange man, as people said—short-tempered yet also rather cold and detached—passionate about some things, but indifferent about most things—determined to make his book and stationery store a success but contemptuous with most customers, and very cynical about human nature. It appeared that he had dragged a step-ladder beneath the beam in the cellar, tied a hemp noose around his neck, climbed up the ladder and kicked the ladder away beneath him—he must have died a horrible, strangulated death, gasping for breath and kicking and writhing for many minutes . . . Seeing the hanged body of my grandfather was one of the terrible shocks of my life. I don't know quite what happened . . . I fainted, I think—then forced myself to crawl to the steps, and made my way upstairs—ran for help . . . I remember screaming on High Street . . . People hurried to help me, I brought them back into the store and down into the cellar, but there was no one there—no rope hanging from the beam, and no overturned step-ladder. Again, it was one of the shocks of my life—I was only eleven, and could not comprehend what was happening . . . Eventually, Grandfather was discovered a few doors away at the Bell, Book & Candle Pub, calmly drinking port and eating a late lunch of pigs' knuckles and sauerkraut. He'd spent most of the day doing inventory, he said, on the second floor of the store, and hadn't heard any commotion.'"

"Poor Amos Slater never entirely recovered from the trauma of seeing his grandfather's hanged body in the cellar of the bookstore, or rather the vision of the hanged body—so everyone who knew him believed . . . ."

"As Milton Rackham reported to me, he'd learned from Amos Slater that the grandfather Barnabas had been a 'devious' person who defrauded business partners, seduced and betrayed naïve, virginal Seabrook women, and, it was charged more than once, 'pilfered' their savings; he'd amassed a collection of first editions and rare books, including a copy of Charles Brockden Brown's *Wieland*—such treasures he claimed to have bought at estate auctions and sales, but some observers believed he had taken advantage of distraught widows and grief-stricken heirs, or possibly he'd stolen outright. Barnabas had married a well-to-do local woman several years his senior to whom he was cruel and coercive, who'd died at the age of fifty-two of 'suspicious' causes. Nothing was *proven*—so Amos Slater had been told. 'Growing up, I had to see how my father was intimidated by my grandfather Barnabas, who mocked him as 'less than a man' for not standing up to him. 'Where is the son and heir whom I deserve? Who are these weaklings who surround me?'—the old man would rage. Grandfather Barnabas was one to play practical jokes on friends and enemies alike; he had a particularly nasty trick of giving people sweet treats laced with laxatives . . . Once, our minister at the Episcopal church here in Seabrook was stricken with terrible diarrhea during Sunday services, as a consequence of plum tarts Barnabas had given him and his family; another time, my mother, who was Grandfather's daughter-in-law, became deathly sick after drinking apple cider laced with insecticide my grandfather had put in the cider—or so it was suspected. (Eventually, Grandfather admitted to putting 'just a few drops' of DDT into the cider his daughter-in-law would be drinking; he hadn't known it was DDT, he claimed, but had thought it was a liquid laxative. 'In any case, I didn't mean it to be *fatal*.' And he spread his fingers, and laughed—it was blood-chilling to hear him.)

Yet, Barnabas Slater had an 'obsessive love' of books—mystery-detective books, crime books—and had actually tried to write fiction himself, in the mode of Edgar Allan Poe, it was said.

"Amos Slater told Rackham that he'd wanted to flee Seabrook and the ghastly legacy of Barnabas Slater but—somehow—he'd had no choice about taking over his grandfather's bookstore—'When Grandfather died, I was designated his heir in his will. My father was ill by that time, and would not long survive. I felt resigned, and accepted my inheritance, though I knew at the time such an inheritance was like a tombstone—if the tombstone toppled over, and you were not able to climb out of the grave in which you'd been prematurely buried, like one of those victims in Poe... Another cruel thing my grandfather boasted of doing—(who knows if the wicked old man was telling the truth, or merely hoping to upset his listeners)—was experimentation with exotic toxins: extracting venom from poisonous frogs that was a colorless, tasteless, odorless, milky liquid that could be added to liquids like hot chocolate and hot coffee without being detected ... The frogs are known as Poison Dart Frogs, found in the United States in the Florida Everglades, it is said ...

"'The Poison Dart Frog's venom is so rare, no coroner or pathologist could identify it even if there were any suspicion of foul play—which there wasn't likely to be. A victim's symptoms did not arouse suspicion. Within minutes (as Grandfather boasted) the venom begins to attack the central nervous system—the afflicted one shivers, and shudders, and can't seem to swallow, for his mouth is very dry; soon, hallucinations begin; and paralysis and coma; within eight to ten hours, the body's organs begin to break down, slowly at first and then rapidly, by which time the victim is unconscious and unaware of what is happening to him. Liver, kidneys, lungs, heart, brain—all collapse from within. If observed, the victim seems to be suffering some sort of attack—heart attack, stroke—'fainting'—there are no gastric-intestinal symptoms, no horrible attacks of vomiting. If the stomach is pumped, there is nothing—no 'food poisoning.' The victim simply fades away ... it is a merciful death, as deaths go.'" Aaron Neuhaus pauses as if the words he is recounting, with seeming precision, from memories of long ago, are almost too much for him to absorb.

"Then, Milton Rackham continued—'The irony is, as Slater told it, after a long and surprisingly successful life as a small town bookseller of quality books, Barnabas Slater did hang himself, it was surmised out of boredom and self-disgust at the age of seventy-two—in the cellar of Slater's Books exactly as his grandson Amos had envisioned. Scattered below his hanging body were carefully typed, heavily edited manuscript pages of what appeared to be several mystery-detective novels—no one ever made the effort of collating the pages and reading them. It was a family decision to inter the unpublished manuscripts with Grandfather.'"

"Isn't this tale amazing? Have you ever heard anything so bizarre, Charles? I mean—in actual life? In utter solemnity poor Milton Rackham recounted it to me, as he'd heard it from Amos Slater. I could sympathize that Rackham was a nervous wreck—he was concerned that his son might do violence against him, and he had to contend with being the proprietor of a store in which a previous proprietor had hanged himself! He went on to say, as Slater had told him, that it had been the consensus in Seabrook that no one knew if Barnabas had actually poisoned anyone fatally—he'd played his little pranks with laxatives and insecticide—but the 'Poison Dart Frog venom' was less evident. Though people did die of somewhat mysterious 'natural causes,' in the Slater family, from time to time. Several persons who knew Barnabas well said that the old man had often said that there are some human beings so vile, they don't deserve to live; but he'd also said, with a puckish wink, that he 'eradicated' people for no particular reason, at times. 'Good, not-so-good, evil'— the classic murderer does not discriminate. Barnabas particularly admired the de Quincy essay 'On Murder Considered One of the Fine Arts' that makes the point that no reason is required for murder, in fact to have a reason is to be rather vulgar—so Barnabas believed also. Excuse me, Charles? Is something wrong?"

"Why, I—I am—utterly confused..."

"Have you lost your way? My predecessor was Milton Rackham, from whom I bought this property; his predecessor was Amos

Slater, from whom he, Rackham, bought the property; and *his predecessor* was a gentleman named Barnabas Slater who seems to have hanged himself in the cellar here—for which reason, as I'd mentioned a few minutes ago, I try to avoid the damned place, as much as possible. (I send my employees down, instead! They don't mind.) I think you were reacting to Barnabas Slater's philosophy, that no reason is required for murder, especially for murder as an 'art form.'"

"But—why would anyone kill for no reason?"

"Why would anyone kill *for a reason*?" Neuhaus smiles, eloquently. "It seems to me, Slater's grandfather Barnabas may have extracted the essence of 'mystery' from life, as he was said to have extracted venom from the venomous frog. The act of killing is complete in itself, and requires no reason—like any work of art. Yet, if one is looking for a reason, one is likely to kill to protect oneself—one's territory. Our ancestors were fearful and distrustful of enemies, strangers—they were 'xenophobic'—'paranoid.' If a stranger comes into your territory, and behaves with sinister intent, or even behaves without sinister intent, you are probably better off dispatching him than trying to comprehend him, and possibly making a fatal mistake. In the distant past, before God was love, such mistakes could lead to the extinction of an entire species—so it is that *Homo sapiens*, the preemptive species, prefers to err by over-caution, not under-caution."

I am utterly confounded by these words, spoken by my affable companion in a matter-of-fact voice. And that smile!—it is so boyish, and magnanimous. Almost, I can't speak, but stutter feebly.

"That is a—a—surprising thing to say, for you . . . Aaron. That is a somewhat cynical thing to say, I think . . ."

Aaron Neuhaus smiles as if, another time, I am a very foolish person whom he must humor. "Not at all 'cynical,' Charles—why would you think so? If you are an aficionado of mystery-detective-crime fiction, you know that someone, in fact many people, and many of them 'innocent,' must die for the sake of the art—for *mystery's sake*. That is the bedrock of our business: Mystery, Inc. Some of us are booksellers, and some of us are consumers, or are consumed. But all of us have our place in the noble trade."

There is a ringing in my ears. My mouth is so very dry, it is virtually impossible to swallow. My teeth are chattering for I am very cold. Except for its frothy remains, my second cup of cappuccino is empty—I have set it on Neuhaus's desk, but so shakily that it nearly falls over.

Neuhaus regards me closely with concerned eyes. On his desk, the carved ebony raven is regarding me as well. Eyes very sharp! I am shivering—despite the heat from the fire. I am very cold—except the whiskers on my jaws feel very hot. I am thinking that I must protect myself—the box of Lindt's chocolate truffles is my weapon, but I am not sure how to employ it. Several of the chocolate truffles are gone, but the box is otherwise full; many remain yet to be eaten.

I know that I have been dismissed. I must leave—it is time.

I am on my feet. But I am feeling weak, unreal. The bookseller escorts me out of his office, graciously murmuring, "You are leaving, Charles? Yes, it is getting late. You might come by at another time, and we can see about these purchases of yours. And bring a check—please. Take care on the stairs!—a spiral staircase can be treacherous." My companion has been very kind even in dismissing me, and has put the attaché case into my hands.

How eager I am to leave this hellish, airless place! I am gripping the railing of the spiral staircase, but having difficulty descending. Like a dark rose a vertigo is opening in my brain. My mouth is very dry and also very cold and numb—my tongue feels as if it is swollen, and without sensation. My breath comes ever more quickly, yet without bringing oxygen to my brain. In the semi-darkness my legs seem to buckle and I fall—I am falling, helpless as a rag doll—down the remainder of the metal stairs, wincing with pain.

Above me, two flights up, a man is calling with what sounds like genuine concern—"Charles? Are you all right? Do you need help?"

"No! No thank you— *I do not . . .*"

My voice is hoarse, my words are hardly audible.

Outside, I am temporarily revived by cold,

fresh wind from the ocean. There is the smell and taste of the ocean. Thank God! I will be all right now, I think. I am safe now, I will escape . . . I've left the Lindt chocolates behind, so perhaps—(the predator's thoughts come frantically now)—the poison will have its effect, whether I am able to benefit from it or not.

In the freezing air of my vehicle, with numbed fingers I am jamming a misshapen key into the slot of the ignition that appears to be too small for it. How can this be? I don't understand.

Yet, eventually, as in a dream of dogged persistence, the key goes into the slot, and the engine comes reluctantly to life.

Alongside the moonstruck Atlantic I am driving on a two-lane highway. If I am driving, I must be all right. My hands grip the steering wheel that seems to be moving—wonderfully—of its own volition. A strange, fierce, icy-cold paralysis is blooming in my brain, in my spinal chord, in all the nerves of my body, that is so fascinating to me, my eyes begin to close, to savor it.

Am I asleep? Am I sleeping while driving? Have I never left the place in which I dwell and have I dreamt my visit to Mystery, Inc. in Seabrook, New Hampshire? I have plotted my assault upon the legendary Aaron Neuhaus of Mystery, Inc. Books—I have injected the chocolate truffles with the care of a malevolent surgeon—how is it possible that I might fail? *I cannot fail.*

But now I realize—to my horror—I have no idea in which direction I am driving. I should be headed south, I think—the Atlantic should be on my left. But cold moon-glittering waters lap dangerously high on both sides of the highway. Churning waves have begun to rush across the road, into which I have no choice but to drive.